# Crazy Alice

By the same author

*Every Twinge a Verdict*
*Green Snake Riding*
*Part of the Deeper Sea*
*This is a Story You Already Know*

# Crazy Alice

second edition

*Lois Marie Harrod*

**Belle Mead Press**
Belle Mead, New Jersey, 1999

## ACKNOWLEDGEMENTS

Acknowledgement is made to the editors of the following magazines in which these poems (some in slightly altered versions) appeared: "And These Beds," *Journal of New Jersey Poets;* "And These Few Precepts," *Ambergris;* "Ars Moriendi," *Black River Review;* "Common Rock," *The Literary Review;* "Crazy Alice," *South Trenton Review;* "Crazy Woman Creek," *Oxford Magazine;* "Dust," *South Trenton Review;* "Elegy for My Virginity," *Journal of New Jersey Poets;* "Endymion," *Visions International;* "Everything Continues," *Zone 3;* "He Enjoins Her to Be Quiet," *Pearl;* "Lazarus," *Phoenix;* "Letter from Ithaca," *The And Review;* "Lies to My Lover," *Zone 3;* "Loving a Sick Woman," *South Trenton Review;* "Moving Out," *The Plastic Tower;* "Nothing Can Be Rushed," *Hiram Poetry Review;* " Ontogeny Repeats Philogeny," *Footwork;* "Sex Without Words," *Palanquin Pamphlet Series;* "Stocking Shelves," *Zone 3;* "The Backwardness of Things" (as "A Posteriori"), *Journal of New Jersey Poets;* "The Ceremony of Running High," *South Trenton Review;* "The End of the Affair," *Pennsylvania English;* "The Failure of Imagination," *Poetry Center Anthology;* "The Roller Skating Rink," *Pearl;* "The Woman Who Became a Tree," *South Trenton Review;* "There Will Be Days," *Ambergris;* "Whitsuntide," *Birmingham Poetry Review;* "Winslow Homer's Two Birds Shot in Flight," *Green Mountains Review.*

I wish to express my deep gratitude to my editor Herman M. Ward.

Second Edition
1999

CRAZY ALICE. Copyright © l991, 1999 by Lois Marie Harrod. All rights reserved. Printed and bound in the United States of America. For information, address Belle Mead Press, 306 Dutchtown Road, Belle Mead, NJ 08502.

Library of Congress Catalog Card Number: 90-084847
ISBN 1-879462-04-4

*for Lee*

TABLE OF CONTENTS

CRAZY ALICE
    Crazy Alice  3
    There Will Be Days  4
    That Day We Caught Bass  6
    Loving a Sick Woman  7
    Stocking Shelves  8
    Elegy for My Virginity  9
    The Failure of Imagination  11
    Ontogeny Repeats Phylogeny  12
    Dirge for the Self I Hung Last Night from the Attic Rafter  14
    Everything Continues  16

SEX WITHOUT WORDS
    Sex Without Words  19
    He Enjoins Her to Be Quiet  21
    Lies to a Lover  22
    When She Could Remember . . .  23
    And These Beds  24
    The End of an Affair  25
    Common Rock  26
    Cow Dream  27
    The Shroud of Turin  28
    The Dung Beetles  29
    Driving East Through South Dakota  31
    Flight  32
    Examining My Breasts  33
    Lightning  34
    I Am Writing Poems Where You Can't Miss Them  35
    Rescue  36
    Preserving the Dark  37

Letter from Ithaca   38
The Return of Ulysses   39
The Woman Who Became a Tree   40
Putting Your Man Back Together   41
How Time Lies in Love   43
Despair   44
Extinct Birds   45
Rest Area   47
Dust   50

ARTIFACTS
Artifacts   53
The Ceremony of Running High   54
Blue Hole, Ohio   58
Cellar   60
Honey Carcass   62
The Chemistry of Self-Healing   63
Like the Gentle Rain   65
Writing on the Inside of a Mobius Strip   66
Crazy Woman Creek, Wyoming   67
High Places   68
Vessels   69
The Roller Skating Rink   70
Fitting Room   71
Moving Out   73
Rest Stop, Memorial Day, 1990   74
The Clarity of Deceit   76
Endymion   77
"I'm Gonna Drive Somewhere Far"   78
"And These Few Precepts"   79
To David, a Student   80
Lazarus   81
Dryope   83
Ars Moriendi   84
Nothing Can Be Rushed   85
The Backwardness of Things   86
Rooming with Women   87
Winslow Homer's Two Birds Shot in Flight   88
Whitsuntide   89

# Crazy Alice

*and this time, Alice, I have the key*

# CRAZY ALICE

Crazy Alice, sitting at our kitchen table
with the sun slipping down your back,
my mother is telling you to go home.
Your hands stuff bones
in the mouth of the kitchen clock.
You took my blue pencil.

Crazy Alice, my mother says you wear feed sacks,
and now she's saying it's dark out there
and I can see the stars are swimming in black cream,
and, Crazy Alice, you better walk back home
where your mama sits at her sewing machine.
And Crazy Alice, I'm going to tell you again
what my mother lets you say, but won't let me.

Crazy Alice, I remember the day in church
you unbuttoned your dress during the sermon
and showed me the big moles whispering to your
    mamas
and my barrette digging through your hair.
I remember your knees knocking down the hymnals
as my mother marched you out.

Crazy Alice, I know the knobs on your knees
are handles to little drawers
where you have hidden my ribbons and combs,
and I know inside that big knuckle of yours
that raps on the kitchen table is a hook
that dangles my music box key,
and, Crazy Alice, I know you're never going home,
and I'm telling you again loud so my mama can hear,
the bogey man is coming, and he's going to get you,
and he's going to open every drawer in your dresser,
and, this time, Alice, I have the key.

# THERE WILL BE DAYS

On the last morning of my childhood
I sucked the salt from the earpieces of my glasses
and talked to Howard Seales about bananas
until Mrs. McKay told me to get right to work,
and Howard said he was only giving me a pencil.

And at the last lunch of my childhood
I watched Jeffrey Martin—
who every mother said
was terribly spoiled and raised by the book—
smash his white bread and mashed potatoes
into his brown hamburger gravy,
and his green peas and his red jello
and all his chocolate milk
into one gray lump
and then eat it to please us all.

And on the last afternoon of my childhood
I sweated through the Virginia Reel
in the elementary gymnasium,
slippering hands with my first and fat boyfriend
    George,
whom I never admitted to anyone
and whom I never called from an all-night party
to ask if his refrigerator was running
or if he had Prince Albert in a can.

And on the last afternoon of my childhood
I walked home with Maggie Flanagan
whose father was already crazy with Huntington's
    disease,
and she would be too,
but then she was fat and telling the number
of calories in one tablespoon
of Aunt Jemima's syrup.

And on the last afternoon
I dawdled with her at the corner

planning how I would stop drinking milk
if there were 160 calories in every cup
until I had to prance home to the toilet.

And on the last day of my childhood
I did not yet know
how a spot of brown blood
would mean start and finish,
clean and dirty,
pleasure and pain;
I did not know
how my months would be measured
and how my mother would say
now there will be days when you can not swim.

# THAT DAY WE CAUGHT BASS

Going with Matty was less like fishing
than a way of catching discarded lines
straggling from willows. We didn't set out to angle,
nor were we like boys—prepared:
    she had a feel for the invisible,
      the way a woman running her finger up her neck
    snags a hair.

Once she found her line, everything else appeared—
rod, bobbin, sinker, fly, hook, worm,
    and then we sat on the wooden bridge,
    baiting our legs in the water.

The day the bass astonished us on a rusty barb
that she had shaken from a beer can,
we planned the whole mile home
    how we would cook it wrapped in wet leaves,
    how we would eat,

but her father, worrying his martini
between clipped nails, said no, not his daughter:
    didn't we know toxins leeched into that lake,
    the fish would make us sick.

So she hid it deep, the old bottom feeder,
down in the garden, below the green tomatoes,
and went inside to pluck her eyebrows:
    I walked home alone,
      pulling at every loose end.

# LOVING A SICK WOMAN

I do not remember what disease she had
or why I had to clean her house,
or why her tight-bloused daughter
with tits like bombs couldn't do it.
She didn't pay and I wasn't compassionate.
Perhaps my father said I must—
he was made of such charity.

But I do remember pushing the carpet sweeper
around her room, nicking the straightback chair
draped with a man's pants, zipper splayed,
down on my knees under the bed holding my breath
against the dust and her flesh
as one does turning into sick rooms
or walking down the road and suddenly seeing
a dead animal in the nettles.

I breathed through my teeth
as she lay on the rancid bed,
asking me the usual questions about school
as if I could not notice
her pillow crossed with black hair—
I tried to move my tongue.

I touched all the ointments and medicines
on her dresser, shaking out the doilies, trying to wipe
the vaseline from the lip of a great blue jar, seeing
a man's claw marks there, knowing
that in all this grease and sickness,
someone was making love to her,
knowing with uncertain grace
that men and women did strange things together
and that this, too, was contagious.

## STOCKING SHELVES

I was sixteen and stocking manicure scissors
and sanitary products at the back of Fetterlein's
    Pharmacy
while Anne Gorgon, age 46, sold Frank Percy
his dirty Coronas up front.

After she fondled his change, she splayed
her careful nails on the Timex case
and gaggled until the customers cleared
their throats.

Up the aisle from the milk of magnesia
I could watch her left mouth moon;
below the perfume, her right lips
hung listless on his words.
She had broken her jaw in a car crash.

The pharmacist told me while I dusted the perms
that the nerves were severed,
but Anne said, adjusting her lipstick in a hand mirror,
that she didn't have headaches anymore.

One Saturday in August she married Frank Percy
and they puffed off to Florida in a haze of cigar.
I asked my mother was it possible, they were so old,
how could they, with one half of her face stone.

All that honeymoon I sold Havanas up front
and John Grenner, pimples masked in pink clay,
bought six chocolate bars, one hour right after
    another,
until he had the nerve
to ask if I didn't know him from somewhere.

# ELEGY FOR MY VIRGINITY

My sister was ten
when Candy McClain showed her 17 ways to do it,
all illustrated, in the book she found
under her parents' bed.

I was twelve when I read
*What Every Young Man Should Know,*
how copper spots would blotch my body
and the bones slough out through my belly
and I would go mad.
I put the book back on the shelf.

So there were things I didn't know in high school,
like the word *fuck*, for example, turning to the boy
who brought me to the basketball game
and asking what was he saying.
My sister hysterical, didn't I ever see
the writing on the bathroom walls?
I knew what happened,
but how could I know what it meant?

Then all those tests I failed—
has a boy ever kissed your
cheek, mouth, ear, neck, nipple, navel?
Has he put his tongue in your teeth?
Have you gone all the way?
And always the laughter, Jesus Christ,
she's whiter than snow.

Then I wanted to die quickly,
the way one wants a parent to go,
so there is no fuss about it,
and it was going to be beautiful,
like first communion.

And I am still waiting for the real loss,
you know, the way the sex therapists say it happens,
complete loss of consciousness for five or six hours,

and be sure to turn off the motor of your car
before you start.

So this is premature,
like the elegy I began for my aunt while she lay
    upstairs dying
and didn't finish when she finally did,

and I can keep you alive, a long time yet,
the way prostitutes do
by a bladder of pig's blood
under the sheet.

And even if you do die,
it will be like Hitler or Elvis,
and I will always be resurrecting you
in Brazil or in some secret vault
in Graceland.

# THE FAILURE OF IMAGINATION

When Angie was fifteen, her pony Boy
threw her into the hospital for three weeks,
heaving her off his back, then stamping her ribs,
her brother wanted to shoot him
with the rifle she had shown me in the barn,
but I whom she made brave, teaching me to ride bareback
    behind her,
my arms locking her waist, legs pressing the coarse flank
    hair,
rode fearless that pony's back the next summer
down through the white pines and past the spring
where she drank with her horses,
and told me again how someone came
at Christmas to steal trees.

Three summers later, when she and I worked
in a rest home and the old man with gouty ankles
kept begging kisses, we told each other
all our secrets, and it wasn't the pony who kicked her, but
    her father—
and I, who had learned to ride the four-legged beast,
could smell that man sitting behind me every Sunday in the
    pew,
his tall face slack as the bridles still hanging on the barn
    wall,
and I could feel his "Father, for the gifts . . ."
slicing the roast that she asked me to share each Sunday,
and I could hear my father quoting him each Tuesday
after the school board met.

At the end of the summer we returned to college,
never seeing each other much again, but when I thought of
    her,
I could see no more than a photograph, her body curled
on the black and white dining room tiles, her face unseen,
and her father's black shoe blurring the top of the picture
like an inadvertent thumb, unfocused, never quite reaching
    her ribs.

# ONTOGENY REPEATS PHYLOGENY

Looking back on her life
as if the Big Bang were the night in which she was
    conceived
and all her life a slow evolution to humanity,
she knew there were alarm clocks she could not
    remember—
the first damp nights in chaos
and the sloshing across the face of the deep.

For a long time she was no more separate
than blue-green algae from lightning
or cockroach from stone.

You are cold fish, he said, early on,
and she was silent turning her neck away from him in
    the theater,
but she remembered his nails pinching her forefinger
like the teeth of a coelacanth,
and she left her infertile eggs on the velvet chair,
knowing he would not return.

She became a thing of her own weather,
raining and snowing and often freezing,
and there was no Eden in her temperament ever,
for she knew that losing her virginity
was not going from innocence to sin,
but something else, some evolution without
    knowledge.
The next boy kissed her without closing his eyes,
his mouth pressing hard against her braces,
and she kept her eyes open too
as if she could learn about reptiles
by staring into the eye of the snake.

But he would not have her Catholic and universal
nor she him nor the next
though she lay all night on top of his body
with heavy plates between them,

he quaking like a brontosaurus
separate in his passion
spending his sperm on cotton
and she without a seismograph.
Then a bear showed her
what it was that bears carried below their bellies,
what it was that warm mammals wanted,
holes to enter, places to curl, periods of hibernation
when there was no need to eat,
and yet in her hand he was eel
and his paws turned to water.

She could not know
why the urge in him was so great
and even as she grew gravid
the universe split
and she was still standing on her feet.

So she was angry with all this,
they had told her that childbirth was easy,
but his head was so big that no thinking
could stop the burning
and all chaos was contracting again.
People were talking too,
men and women prophesying
that it was to lose consciousness that she had come to
     this
just as she began to know:
it was the child torching the inside of her belly,
and she could not yet grasp this pleasure
flinging her back to stone.

# DIRGE FOR THE SELF I HUNG LAST NIGHT FROM THE ATTIC RAFTER

*Play a blue song for me,*
*bluer than the bruise of the black blue sky*
*for I have hung myself on a blue black rafter*
*and I am azure through and through—*
*(where there is no air*
*there is only blue).*
*Play a blue song for me.*

She climbed with me the long blue ladder,
we looked each by each
for the laces we used to finger,
the stories we used to wear—
the apron of the queen of hearts
the cape of her knave despair
and the blue blue hair.

We found a blue rope, a silken strand,
and she said to me
there the rafter and there the opening
to the floor below
and nothing but silverfish
to live in the blue, blue hair.
I will die alone
and you can see me swinging
like fresh despair.

*Play a blue song for me,*
*bluer than the bruise of the black blue sky*
*for I have hung myself on a blue black rafter*
*and I am azure through and through—*
*(where there is no air*
*there is only blue).*
*Play a blue song for me.*

You are blue and cold, I said,
with your small feet, blue and cold
and I have not found

the apron of your queen of hearts
or the cape of your knave despair,
only the blue blue air.

*Play a blue song for me,
bluer than the bruise of the black blue sky
for I have hung myself on a blue black rafter
and I am azure through and through—
(where there is no air
there is only blue).
Play a blue song for me.*

## EVERYTHING CONTINUES

Everything continues: your grandfather
is hanging from the rafters in a barn in Carroll
 County
while your grandmother is dying in a rest home in
 Clyde
where she is just opening the barn door,
her apron still wet from the dishes she is washing,
her forefinger still straight though she lies crooked
in her grave in Cincinnati.

In her unforgiving way she is still nesting
her right hand in her left, as if it
were a small bird without feathers
that will someday poke out your eye.

She is still sitting in the pale green chair
between the refrigerator and the telephone,
still chiding you in your pale green prom dress,
still frightened by the whiteness
of your skin.

# Sex Without Words

*those endless variations*

## SEX WITHOUT WORDS

Afterwards, if she asked him what he had been
    thinking,
he always replied that sex was wordless,
that he had not been thinking at all.

Of course, she knew that he did think about it,
but only afterwards. Once, just as he was falling to
    sleep,
he said, "I thought of you during my lecture today,

and for a second I could not speak."
Then she knew that something from the night before
had startled him mid-sentence,

this man for whom words were a public pleasure,
some image like a word unbidden (was it her hand
wiping his thigh, his wrist against her chin?)

and that he had stood there, in his classroom,
before his students as he lay with her,
an animal who could not speak.

Sometimes she tried to remember their first sex,
when she had known so little about pleasing him
and had no words for her own body—

there was a blue quilt, an iron bedstead,
a fan droning the beginning of an alphabet
and he touching her in places without names.

Sometimes she tried to be like him, all body,
to shut off the words that made her flesh and blood,
to be wordless in her coming, the snow leopard

beneath his hand, the white snake,
but always the words came with her,
these are my spots, my claws, this is my skin.

Sometimes she grew angry—why wouldn't he speak?
Nothing of her body repulsed him, nothing of her
   sweat,
her skin, nothing but the naming of it.

Sometimes she wanted him to know
that he was so carnal and pure,
and that she was only a voyeur beside him,

watching his body make love to her
and writing it down in her head.
What if she published those endless variations,

how she was never the same body in the same bed?
There were men too who had to keep their clothes on,
or wanted dirty litanies to keep them hard,

men who needed words as she did,
but not so many and so various—
she did not want such men,

and yet she needed words to love
this man who did not need words,
this man who had refused all words

to be in her bed with her alone.

## HE ENJOINS HER TO BE QUIET

Oh, I've got you by the nape of the neck
the scruff, the scrag, the long goose song
I've got you by the jugulum—
for the love of Pete, come undone,
shut-up and let me love.

Oh, I want you from the latch inside
the buckle-down the tight-up screw
skewer, rivet, fetter, clip
nails and garter, clamp and lip
I want to lock out your voice and lock me in—
oh, you've got me in your heavy metal mouth
like a trumpet blare,
can't you join the long brass note
to silver silence?

Or if you can't be quiet,
let's have a chain of verses,
a refrain twining
ivy over brick,
you the ivy, I the brick,
and the cling between us
the song like sealing wax
a voice, your voice
the lime
the lute

## LIES TO A LOVER

I have seen all things this summer,
honeysuckle thicker than semen,
blue eggs falling
uncracked from the nest,
the turtle humping his steady way
across the tar. Every storm
has delivered bones to read.

I have not imagined the bluebird cutting
the corner of my eye as I dropped your letter
nor the deer staring until the whole woods opened
a peacock's fan.

Why would I lie that the pheasant struts
with his neck in the noose
or that three wild turkeys
made a pompous crossing
to some circumstance in the trees?

This is the truth:
each foot lifted from the gravel
as if the trinity hung in their wings,
a cock and two mistresses.
How could I invent such things?

# WHEN SHE COULD REMEMBER...

She remembered telephone numbers, grocery lists, and the periodic table,
and when he wanted to call his dentist, she gave him the weight of silver in her cavities,
but he had to remind her to fill the car with gas
so that she wouldn't be stranded between High Bridge and Xanadu.

Sometimes she remembered to take out the trash even though she knew the earth was too full
and he worried about bringing in the mail and losing her credit card bill (which was never extravagant
but which she so easily forgot to pay).

Always he liked to fix breakfast because she would forget to eat it,
and she left him for hours until he was sure that she would never return
and when he followed her into the woods he could see that she had gone alone
to hear the Goldberg variations played on stone.

Frequently he liked to be in the same room with her
when she wasn't there, watching over her body
lest she leave it slumped on an ottoman.

Once a day he took it out and dusted it off
so that it would be clean when she returned
and she always sneezed because she had grown allergic to her own skin.
Sometimes he bathed it and held it in his arms
and called her, hoping that she might hear.

When she returned, he asked her where she had been
but she could never tell—
once she said that she thought that she was an apple tree
and he could eat if he wanted
but the fruit was green
and bitter in his mouth.

23

## AND THESE BEDS

Last night as we slept,
this bed took itself
and knocked gently on the bedroom wall
which opened like a bread box
and dropped us into the night,
sheets billowing from our bodies.

Last night it met all the beds
parachuting from all the black rooms,
scraping the earth as all love beds must
like stiff-legged centipedes,

lilting from side to side,
white sheets waving to the stars,
then tossed its sleepers into the air
and held them thread on thread.

Last night this bed lingered until dawn,
planting its four posts in the four corners of the field,
until it branched a full canopy of leaves.

# THE END OF AN AFFAIR

My lover couldn't understand why I glued black
    feathers in my hair
when the crab apples blossomed—
I want to be a raven, I said, as he floated away.
How could I have guessed that he
had been hiding silk wings under our bed?

I had loved him with a serpentine passion
at least half of the time he lived with me,
and he had revealed himself to me every day.
At night we both wet our skins and pinched out the
    candle.

Of course, I went looking for him in all the places
we had hidden from each other: the Chinese take-
    out, the china shop,
certain passages in *Bulfinch's Mythology.*
He wasn't there, but I enjoyed myself
and kept looking.

When I found him at last at the bottom of the
    Hudson,
it took a chainsaw to open his coffin,
but everything was there, even his driver's license,
which I had never seen.
He was only eighteen.
I've brought him back to the apartment
where he has been sitting all night in my reclining
    chair,
the kerosene flickering off his golden horns.

# COMMON ROCK

I know a story
how a man and a woman go fishing.
He wades the stream
flicking the hook from his wrist,
she skirts the edges
picking the stones that please her.

When night comes to rock and water,
they sit in their cabin, sucking rainbows
one by one and the violet bone
always catches in her throat.

Then she shows him the stones she has chosen,
the black flint nested in its white shell, the granite
    egg,
the rain-pocked shale, the honey-combed clay,
the feldspar, the quartz, the limestone with its shallow
    fin.

She kneels before the fire and glazes each one
with her tongue, unafraid, spitting when she has to,
until each shimmers like a fluorescent fish,
and he puts out his hand to touch it too,
marvelling every night as if she has never touched
him this way before.

# COW DREAM

I am heavy with milk
waiting in the meadow
for someone you perhaps
to take the long teats
in the ring of your fingers
and pull.

I can not see your face against me
but your ear rests
on the great cow heart
as you slide down.

In between
I lie in the meadow
hooves folded
under my carcass
chewing on everything
that I have chewed upon
before.

## THE SHROUD OF TURIN

I will pour ink into you
and

lay my paper
over the pocked surface of your face.
I will press my vellum into the gouges of your eyes
and force my rags into your rifts.

I print your body
on white linen.

Years from now
when your sheet curtains some chancel wall
someone will notice
that you are still there
appearing in the chasm of a candle

and they will say
moving the flame from side to side
there is the image of his hand

there is his mouth
and the lips parted
like a girl's.

The experts of heat and light
will appear
and test your age
and explain the chemical formula
by which I printed you
and then
if there are still
lovers and churches
the miracles begin.

And what will it matter then
that you so suffered for me?

# THE DUNG BEETLES

### I.
On the grasslands north of Sheridan
I watched two beetles rolling a pearl of dung.
One braced his forefeet on the ground and pushed,
the other directed, sometimes riding the globe like a
　　circus bear,
sometimes slipping under the sweet stench.

I followed them twenty-five feet on my belly
until my shadow fell over them,
and they let go their earth.

### II.
I wake one morning in warm dung
knowing that I must eat my way to the surface
or die in the egg.

I am the darkness
devouring darkness,
the Cheops
eating my way out of parched wrappings,
I fill my belly with my own skin,
I suck the jelly from my skull.
I swallow all I know.

I am the sacred scarab devouring this rotting earth.
I am the sacred sun.
I am the fire.

### III.
This earth is not something that beetles roll alone,
but all through the spring
coming in pairs like Mormon boys
pumping bicycles, their faces flushed
in the wet sun of May, tasting beliefs
like hard clay tablets on their tongues,
coming in pairs like old women with bad breath

waiting the watchtowers,
knowing as much of evolution
as beetles,
coming like little girls buying diaries
where they practice the words
that will come to flesh.

## IV.
There are three hundred thousand
kinds of beetles and only one of us and not so kind,
so if we learn a lesson from nature
it is this: we can not roll such balls alone.

Coming in pairs like lovers and beetles
we roll the excrement of our continuance
into the eternal egg
more lowly than any manger
and more natural.

# DRIVING EAST THROUGH SOUTH DAKOTA

Two weeks in Wyoming and you could sleep as if time
had something to do with the sun but I woke every morning at
   four,
your watch luminous on the pillow.  I could hear your parents
   hobbling
through the rooms above us,  slinging their bodies
between their crutches.  They do not sleep, you said in the
   light,
as if you had been the one awake.

Now going home we face the gold clock.  You call this losing
   time
and set your watch an hour east before you have to;
I leave mine as it is but it's not absolutes I'm arguing,
only the complicated adjustments.

The children sleep as we drive steadily through the Badlands,
thinking of your parents.  When we reach Murdo,
where time officially jerks back and forth,
you begin talking softly about people who live on the edge:
must they specify central and mountain, do they get confused?
I remember you said the same last year,
and wonder again if time is linear.

Then you assume people more exact than yourself,
ones who pull their cars over to the side of the road
to lose or gain this hour precisely, people ungoverned by body
   or light.
You imagine a restaurant of riches,  hoards of travelers
resetting their stomachs, here, on instant gravy,
but we know time doesn't work that way.
The children sleep, we do not stop.

We pass a motorcyclist with a belly swelling over his waist line,
a truck of tombstones, you talk of Zen and chisels,
and I try to think what time it will be when we all get home.

# FLIGHT

This morning it is important
to tell you that a blue jay
hung himself in my berry netting:
I didn't want to kill him,
only keep our few bushes
from the birds.

He was hungry, he was flying
on the brashest of wings:
he wanted only the fruit below
that something else claimed.

I wanted so little, a patch of berries
and a child who knew the names
of flying things.

I did not tell you then, years ago,
about the black swallowtail
our son swatted into a thistle,
how it hung there framed in flinching,
and I afraid to unpin its wing.

The gloves I have worn
to carry wrens to hedges,
the brooms to sweep down moths,
shovels and tissues to bury dead things,
how can you forgive?

Our son has stopped collecting butterflies.
I do not think I can pull
this last blue thief
from the webbing.

Do not leave.  I can not imagine
what protective gear I would need
to clean up your unfeathering.

# EXAMINING MY BREASTS

These breasts that you love I can not touch.
When the physician asks, do you examine them
    monthly,
I see the diagram in the bottom of my jewelry chest,

a woman stretched on her back, her blue fingers
moving clockwise from her armpits.
The next morning I remember his concerned voice

as I shower: do it now, with soapy fingers,
while there still is time. You are shaving,
you are whistling "La ci darem" in the steam.

There must be others like me, nuns in their baths,
soaping their breasts with washcloths like gloves.
They do not mention lumps in their longest prayers.

The woman who had tuberculosis told my mother
that she would lie out in the sun with her bathing suit
rolled down to her nipples, but she was flat as a man.

The woman with only one breast wore
her white librarian blouse locked to the neck.
It is three weeks before I call for the x-ray:

the white hand plushes my fat between the plastic
    plates,
the white throat apologizes, mammograms,
so uncomfortable, but I do not listen,

this flesh is not mine except those times
when you suck so patiently my milk
comes shuddering up through my body
into my mouth.

## LIGHTNING

Maybe you have heard of hikers
who, taking refuge from a storm,
crawl into a granite cave and are trapped
by the lightning.
They can not get away.

Can you see their bodies unattached to any wire
flipping like phosphorescent fish in a bucket?
Darling, it could rain all night,
and how can I explain?
It's not the mind, and it's not the body.

Some days bolt such agony,
electricity from the starkest blue,
lightning in the safest cavern,
there is no accounting.

You don't have to be standing under a tall tree
or wearing leather shoes,
you can walk backwards
down an unused railroad track,
you can touch an eyelash to the sun:
pain flashes down your skin,
steams off your sweat,
explodes your clothes,
leaves you writhing on the grass,
hair aflame.

Darling, it could rain all day tomorrow,
and how can I explain?

# I AM WRITING POEMS WHERE YOU CAN'T MISS THEM

I'm writing poems where you can't miss them,
in the white margins of your books,
on napkins, lint and cherry pits,
on the icy tablets in your gin.
I've scribbled sonnets in the coal bin of your cabin,
and when you shave my words appear
sharp and steamy in your mirror.
I've wadded a whole volume into your running shoes
which you must read before your socks,
and when you floss, love letters stick
like hooks in rocks.

I am changing the main ingredients of your soup,
your beans will sound of plows and fields and roots.
You won't sleep for the greenstone in your pillow
and I have scrawled shouting stars in the fallow
of your bed.

I've taken your antique desk polished by your
    grandfather
and scratched wings in it, and burned your marble-
    topped table
with a grease pencil and what I have written
on your Dali and Picasso will make you flinch.

There is no stopping me, your body's next.

# RESCUE

This is not rape, you say,
but what lovers do
when there is no shield but flesh
slammed across flesh on some airport floor,

when something wrapped in rags
holds an AK-47 to the skull,
when one is dying and the other must
pump breath back down the throat.

I know tremor racked on tremor,
the clay plates of this earth
buckling until they break,
the aftershock that can not end.

I want a hospital now, I want sleep,
I want as far away from you as I can go
with you thrown over me
like a sheet.

# PRESERVING THE DARK

When his first light filled her mouth,
she dropped her garments at his feet
and could not speak there was such sun.

What did it cost
to live in light,
let him count moths,

wax the moon
until she could watch spiders wrap
silk scarves around the wings of caterpillars.

In morning he asked for nothing
but the bright skin
she gave him.

Then one evening he fell asleep
before lighting the torches,
and all night she lay on a dark bed.

Black palms spangled
her thighs and black panthers
circled the bed posts.

So there must be rules between them,
no searchlights on Tuesdays
and every lamp must wear a hood.

The next day she began
a delicate construction of mirrors
to watch the distant stars.

## LETTER FROM ITHACA

All day the sea littered the beach with unsigned letters
and when the sun spelled your name on the hot water,
my bed scratched across the sand
and floated out towards you.

I lay listening to the great white lies of whales
and heard the gulls panting their alphabet to the
    moon.
I watched for your sails.

At moonlight you began to sweat through my dreams,
your shirts hanging on my bedposts
like white weeds.

Just before dawn you came to my tongue
an emerald flash at the tip of words
and I woke as always
mouth sharp with broken shells.

# THE RETURN OF ULYSSES

The sea had flicked soundless for some time, rumors
    of sharks
had been jerked from the evening news, bluefish
    mouthed
rubber teeth. The house had been quiet,

the son off to second grade where no one mentioned
    jaws ,
and when she picked him up at the soccer field at six,
    she planned
to stop at the supermarket, swordfish for supper.

The bathroom had been so clean, the daughter
    trained to strangle
washcloths and hang them neatly, and even as she
    remembered
that the girl must be finished with her violin lesson
    and waiting,

the hot water beading down her belly did not swell
to a man crawling from the sea like some scaly
    Godzilla.
Nothing predicted his claw upon the knob,

barnacles slipping from his skin, the sheath dissolving,
the soap scudding off his beard, the water ripping his
    thighs
like a dull razor, like a horror she once had known.

# THE WOMAN WHO BECAME A TREE

Since she had become a tree,
a few cells beneath her bark
measured her growing
and rain no longer flooded her cellar.

Her friends said that she
had become, if anything,
more beautiful—of course, her skin
was no longer smooth
and no one expected to caress her.

Her friends considered becoming trees too:
it wasn't expensive
and only the first shot of hormones caused itching.
It certainly lasted longer that a facelift.

Sometimes, though, she thought
she should have chosen something ornamental like a
    yew
or something sturdy like a beech,
something someone could slip a penknife into.

## PUTTING YOUR MAN BACK TOGETHER

It's not easy, putting your man back together.
He's always been dismembered by something sinister,
a sickle-wielding child, a butcher's knife,
a snake-headed woman, a scathing review.

Nor can you just throw all his parts in a pot,
cook three hours and expect him to emerge
maybe a little red like a lobster,
maybe a little tough, but nonetheless a man.

First you have to find him, bit by bit—and that,
    ladies,
is like trying to find fifteen kinds of beans
for some splendid soup that not one of your children
    will eat,
not even the one who wields the sickle.

No, his parts have been hidden
by people you never suspect: the cross-eyed Avon
    lady,
his best friend who puts "For Sale" signs
in your yard every time you go on vacation,

the Amoco attendant with the Irish lilt.
That's why you find the pieces slowly, one by one—
his spleen hidden in the leisure section of the New
    York Times,
his thumb in the center of a chocolate mousse.

Finally, you have everything but the one part that is
    always missing,
the one you would return to him if you could just
    find it,
not because you want more children
but because he looks so silly standing there

his hands pretending to be needed as fig leaves.
He simply can't be allowed to fake it anymore—
so you make him one, a gold one and he likes it.
In fact, he says it is the only thing you've ever given
    him

that he really likes and a month later ,
when you have begin to grow great again,
you can not decide whether it should belong to him
or to this jewel of your own making.

# HOW TIME LIES IN LOVE

At midnight everything moved apart, the raindrops
balled up and scooted individually across the waxed metal,
the acorns dropped plank by plank to the road,
each nailed by a worm, the wind wrote flesh
on the petal of a rose and tore it off sheet by sheet, the
    rabbit sucked
the marigold with a solitary whistle and dropped the
    stems
into the mail slot without addressing one,
she separated the gravel from the dry beans
and glued the stones individually to the inside of her shoe,
and she was separate from him.

At dawn everything hung still, the frog's tongue
fixed the dragonfly at the end of speech
and would not roll him in, the worm steeled
himself against the robin, the sparrow
held like a bomb above her nest, the wind dropped his
    pen
above the catalapa, the cigars meandered
like painted roads, the bacon held its breath
and the fat wouldn't stop burning her arm as she clutched
    the stove,
caught in the anger of turning towards him as the door
    slammed,
and she was separate from him.

At noon, if noon can come when time lies,
everything resumed, the rain its majority, the worm
its belly, the dragonfly its tongue, and the wind
writing one hundred times for his wickedness
the name of the sun in the hot sky. The rabbit puffed at
    his carrot
and the bacon slipped back and forth on the bottom of
    her foot
easing the gravel, and he returned
for lunch with a handful of unaddressed violets, and
she made a salad with blue leaves for both of them to eat,
and she was separate from him.

# DESPAIR

At midnight she had been weeping so long
he told her that she was her own hair shirt,
and she said he was too intellectual
to understand.

He said she should drop it, sink it in the sea,
and she said that her mind was a stone
but her body had no weight.

He wanted to know then what she wanted,
reaching across the bed to her,
running his finger down the small of her back.

How can I make love, he said, when you are crying,
turning from her until she could see his back
twisted in the sheet.

And she knew then
that she must reach for him,
that she must pull him back,
but she could not just then.

# EXTINCT BIRDS

He had loved
the male's scarlet chin
as he tipped his golden bill
to let a drop of water slip
his throat

and she had loved
the female's silver rump
at the base of her ebony tail.

All December
she had waited at the kitchen window
to see the two fluffing
on a leafless branch,
so downy seemed their passion
against the snow.

He had called to her
as they moved towards spring,
come, the birds are feeding now,
see how he offers a sunflower seed,
see how she receives.

At night
she had read to him
from her journal:
all morning the pair
flew back and forth
from their new nest
in the grape arbor
weighed down with
dandelion gauze. . . .

Neither was sure
when they stopped
seeing the birds—
how long had it been?
Maybe a cat, he said one day,

maybe, she said,
and they never
spoke of them again.

# REST AREA

She drops from bright andromedas,
and galaxies of spinning tires,
into the black hole,
cool and dank,
where she peers
at the pale spectre
of herself
on the restroom wall.
*Mirror stainless.*

*Take off your sunglasses,*
tendrils of toilet paper
all the way back
to the last stall,
where **I would like to suck your**
women calling to each other,
"Gloria is that you?"
*Must be that bus I passed*
*from Solid Rock I built . . . Myself,*
"Anne, do you have any paper in yours?"
*Half a roll* "It's me, Blanche, and there ain't none
in here . . ." someone without a name
singing in the stall next to her,
large leather sandals
flapping up and down the dirty tile,
purple lipstick **Don and Cindy,**
large and luminous
on the door before,
someone singing
in violet notes,
large and luminous
as her feet flapping
"What a friend we have in . . ."
**Lyn and Keith** *and the man*
*who took her blood*
*in the cafeteria*
*of the high school*

where she taught until June,
singing *like the maroon lipstick on*
**Deposit soiled napkins here**
*and all the time her maroon blood
flowing from the large vein
in her forearm,
large like her mother's,*
**Lucille and Gotshall,**
*the vein visible even
in her wedding picture, bulging below
the puffed sleeve of her white dress,
so easy to take blood from me,*
"Do you know," she heard herself ask
the phlebotomist, *"do you know
'There is a Fountain Filled with Blood'"?*
and the phlebotomist did *"all our sins and griefs to
    bear"*
he was a Baptist from Tennessee
and he sang it for her
there in the high school cafeteria
with two of her students lying to the right and the left
**Jen and Frankie** squeezing out their blood,
*"There is a fountain filled with blood
flowing from our Savior's side,"*
singing it to a new tune,
not the one John had sung
and not with John's laughter,
**FOOLS NAMES LIKE FOOLS**
*asses, I can't sit here,*
"bring it to the Lord in prayer,"
and the heavy smear of bright bloodstick
**Mary and** . . . *I must have
blood on my purse,*
and she began singing
as she poised over the stool
another song he had taught her
*"We never eat fruitcake
cause fruitcake has rum
and one little bite"*

balancing herself forward
afraid to sit down
*"one little bite
turns a man to a bum."*

## DUST

All night the dust made soft mounds on my skin
and silked between my fingers; it hung in the air
    above your beard
like a dingy veil. I spread wet sheets in the windows,
and wore wet cotton across my face,
but the night grew so thick, I could not breathe.
When I opened my mouth to call your name,
my tongue plowed a clay field. I watched the man I
    used to love
walk past the shed, kicking fine smoke
as high as his hips; the dust filled the hollow of his
    back
like a river. I followed a flight of jackrabbits
smudging the moonlight, and when you woke,
the only white spot was where you laid your head.

# Artifacts

*into the dark with my skulls by the bushels*

# ARTIFACTS

I'm out there in my t-shirt and jeans in the dry field,
desecrating dust, shovel after shovel, all the things I've laid to rest:
the infant sucking silver beads, broken bowls, pumpkin seeds,
the filigreed cross dropped by some wandering missionary,
the girl hiding her teeth in an ancient reliquary, who knows the
    date,
the boy whose skull I smashed, the jawbone of an antique ass,
the man (who would not have me) gored by a bull—
all in my tent, the skulls lined up like molars,
sockets tilted towards the sun.

What relatives I have picket the mounds, swig beer at the holes
    I've dug,
they throw their children in front of my pick-up truck to stop me,
they storm my shack and steal femora and tibiae to stake their
    dahlias.
Their lawyers have discovered legal loopholes, they say,
the sacredness of time and the profanity of space.
What is wrong with me, they ask, have I no religion,
and why can't I sell these things for cash.

Archaeologists come at dusk with flashlights,
they moan that I'm not careful, I don't calibrate the Clovis points,
I haven't laid out my dig in straight lines, I haven't separated the
    coarse from the fine,
and when will I get around to carbondating my bone marrow?

They don't understand why I have to touch the artifacts every day,
things disintegrate with so much handling,
they want to lock everything from me in steel drawers and glass
    cases,
they want me to claim, once and for all,
this was the plastic bracelet I wore—and not my sister.

It's back to the field again, into the dark with my skulls by the
    bushels,
it's toss and tractor—it's spring, plow them in,
let wheat grow between my teeth.

# THE CEREMONY OF RUNNING HIGH

Wake
as the sun snorts the thin white line
between the blind
and window sill,
slip
into your skin as if your shorts,
your feet as if your running shoes,
stuff
a ten dollar bill into your pocket.
Leave him languid behind you,
his beard curled in his dreams.
Go alone.

Lift
your arms to rattle
the mourning dove nesting
in the oak,
leap
the porch
like a moon flower trumpeting.

Lope
gently at first
past the telephone pole
where the orange Crayola
has left this month
everyday its message:
*LOST
BLACK AND WHITE KITTEN
NAMED OREO*

Sing
a song to your ears,
*Mine eyes have seen*
the ebony,
*mine eyes have seen*
the suckle,
the mangle of honey

the blossom and black vine.

Pock
the puddle
where the gravel shimmers,
pock
the sand still singing
until the dogs at Cokey's Kennels
yowl to sink their teeth in you.
You are their matins,
their morning prayer.

Sing
a song in your knees,
in your bowels,
sing
the long pant
up Van Dyke Road,
sing
though you can't lift
your feet, your eyes,
shorten your steps,
ascend,
sing
to the gutter,
to the trickle of silver thistle,
to the broken bottle of Old German in the wild oats,
to the centerfold of *Playboy*, nipples fading in the sun,
to the pantyhose flung on the blackberry briar,
to the pint of J. B.,
to the red t-shirt *Life is a Beach,*
to the empty Big Mac,
to the Nike torn at the tongue.
Sing
as you pitch the bit of fur
orange and white
into the soybeans,
don't stumble,
sing as you heave,
sweat stinging down your thighs.

Clench
the vein in your temple,
clutch
the ice to your eye,
hold
the pulse from migraine,
keep
the stomach sweet,
keep,
the vein from dilating,
stay, you can,
the pain.

Reach,
reach
the top of the hill,
hit,
hit,
the meadows sharpen,
maples shimmer, the sun grows orange,
roses needle, the sky-blue thorn,
you've run the worst to bright downhill.
You are high with running,
with blood splashing,
with body like a waterfall,
you are past pain
and seeing clearly all the way
across the valley
to Greenwood Cemetery,
where the tombstones read
*Richard David Frauendorf Age 18,*
you can see the strawberry plants
beyond the grave
where the seeded hearts hang.

Run
run
down the valley,
run
run
to pick up the milk,
spin
into Krauszer's breathless,
float
over the dirty tile,
float
where *The Times* lies ripping,
float
where the styrofoam cups smell of snow,
and the cashier says:

"What bright eyes—
and so early in the morning."

## BLUE HOLE, OHIO

I am the wet eye,
the watery rent in the universe.
Walk around the shaky planks,
stare in, the water is clear as a fish tank,
you can see the blue ledge, corrugated,
miles down, boys are tossing in
pennies, girls their silver rings, no one knows
how they fall.

They send down divers every year,
army corps with bell jars
and steel instruments,
accurate, circumspect.
The earth is deeper here
than elsewhere, they say,
she should have a hot center,
but we haven't reached warm water
and we are half-way to the moon.

They bring school girls
clutching wet pears in brown paper sacks,
school boys suckling cartons of milk,
they let them take off their canvas shoes
and slip in one by one.
The boys whistle to each other
like whales wheeling in orderly gyres.
No one pushes.

The lines above grow longer and longer,
grown men and women walk around
on new  aluminum ramps,
all waiting to enter the water.
They wear their patent leather shoes,
their Sunday clothes,
white-haired women their white gloves,
white-haired men their silver canes.
They call to each other as they descend,
blisters rising from their lips

like hymns.
Their clothes dissolve,
their bodies bleach,
their skin comes white
and then translucent
like glass shrimp.
They whisper darkly between the verses
where is the end?

Kings and queens and presidents wait
on the rust-proof ramp to begin their haughty
    descent,
rolling out red carpet as they go,
rubies rising to the surface.

I take in thousands
and thousands.
The whole population of the earth
steps into me
and spirals down
as neatly as a notebook.

There are not enough people
on this planet
to fill me.

We should cover her,
a few begin to say,
such a blue gaping,
we should drain her,
we should freeze her
solid to the core.

It is a good idea
but no one knows how.

## CELLAR

Things were falling to sleep in her cellar, she guessed,
but it hadn't lost its darkness nor its rankness,
rank as a bitch, she said, tucking in her breath,
she didn't have to go there, what was the sense?
what could it hold for her anymore?

She took the ammonia and broom and descended the
    stairs,
she could get the place cleaned out once and for all,
disinfect things—one last blood-bath and that would
    be it.

Of course, it hadn't come to that yet—
she calculated her chances,
one in ten, high, of course,
but what with radon seeping up through the cracks,
she should have had it tested.

Silly, she said, no egg no chicken, that's it.
No supermarket tabloid
was going to make a fool of her,
the rivers had shifted
and the ground was drying up,
the odors, the roots,
the dankness, the white beetle
had taken up residence elsewhere.
Where could they go?
It was not as if
one could just tunnel from room to room.
There was nothing she could smell.

It must be hibernation then she thought,
the beetle sleeps,
the snail no longer keeps company.

There had always been a slug or two,
no matter how often she scrubbed,
and now she could still pick up a transparent trail

with her flashlight.
She felt she could love this one
not touching it, but following
its paper luminescence into the woodwork.
She would not have to pull it from the bottom of her
    foot,
she could just let its horns
move across the clay,
glad  something
had a little slime left.

# HONEY CARCASS

*And I came at last to my carcass in the weeds
and lo, bees, had built a honeycomb in my ribs.*

And she knew at last what the wise woman warned:
how she must hold him in a small ring
and bear his burning,
how she must walk
after the ravage and not scream,
how she must arch against him,
and not let go.

Within her, the volcano, the hundred-armed monster,
the wrench, the sword, the mace, the all
until his strength gave to gentle rain.

In time the thigh of heaven would plead for mercy—
and he would yield up his secrets:
he would grant that she too
could leave her carcass
by the side of the road
until the bees take up a habitation
and begin to sing.

# THE CHEMISTRY OF SELF-HEALING

It's World War II, things go hard:
the cock struts among the chicks,
the hen squawks, legs soften in the ditch.

You're safe in the belly,
the shell forming around you.
The egg tightens,
you're squeezed onto hay.

Another world and more of the same:
the air cuts, the fingers rasp,
the gold ring taps the calcium,
you smell cabbage and gasoline,
you hear the voice of Rita Levi-Montalcini
in the street market
asking if you're fertilized.

Her delicate fingers wrap around you,
she lays you in her basket and takes you
to her tiny apartment
where she pillows you under her bed lamp.
You relax, you are warm.
you form a heavy head,
your eyes dig in.

One day, are you listening, she snips you open
with her manicuring scissors
and twists off your wings.
She puts you in a jar
and flies to St. Louis where
she implants mouse tumors
at your shoulders and hips.

Now here is the strange part:
you grow—those nerves of yours,
those tentacles,
grow right into the tumor
where your wings ought to be.

You probe your pain.

But she is not satisfied,
she tears your limbs again,
she stains your nerves,
she maps your body.
You find a new way to invade your tumors,
to force your vessels,
to wrestle your blood.
This is knowledge
and she wants more.
It must be the cancer itself that makes you grow.

She drops just one of your nerve ganglia
into the culture dish with tumor cells,
where in only ten hours
you grow a "dense halo of nerve fibers,
radiating out like rays from the sun"
in the catalyst of your own destruction.

## LIKE THE GENTLE RAIN

One day that summer
when the heat was a gnat in her eye,
the haze began to sweat,
big drops at first, shaken by crows,
splatting on her forehead,
but as she reached the last woodland,
where the paved road muddied into gravel
and tunneled through the sassafras to the top,
her hair whipped her face in the downdraft
and her hips came sore riding the ruts.

Then the rain began so slow and fine
that she hardly knew it at first from her own salt,
and continued, the wind ceasing
and her body growing steady against the incline.
The rain nuzzled inside her t-shirt, licking her nipples
and her thighs rose and fell wet too,
and the rain clung to her, not in a hot drenching
but a gentle skinning
of her own nakedness.

## WRITING ON THE INSIDE OF A MOBIUS STRIP
(for Gina)

By the time I reach my house,
the paper has twisted my nothingness out,
I pull myself along on a warm leash.

My neighbor's dog knows right away
that I am not the woman who lived next door,
he leaps the hedge to nuzzle my thigh.
He barks at the new smell of me.

How he rolls in the grass now that I have become
    man,
how he brings me his ball, his stick, his rubber bone,
all the little boys sing from the top of their swings
that I am one of them.

We dance, we yap, we flick our paper swords in the
    wind,
no one watches from their dining room window,
no one shouts *creep* or *pervert, unfit to be with
    children,*
no one cares that I have turned myself inside out.

In an hour or two I get tired of pawing their rabbit
    holes,
tired of barking their dogged little songs,
tired of dangling too much in the sun.

I worry about burning and bruising the delicate skin.
I turn myself into myself again,
twisting my nothingness in.

# CRAZY WOMAN CREEK, WYOMING

When she came here, it was wagon be damned I'll
    bathe
and she shredded the ginghams from her waist
and stood naked in the dry river bed.

Bring me my soap, she said, the stuff I made
from fat and lye, for I will wash here with white birds,
and the men could not stop her and looked away.

What children there were watched between their
    fingers
and the bravest threw off his hat and danced in the
    dust
until he could taste the stuff from which he was made.

As the moon rose, she sang softly to the wagons,
bring the water now, for I must rinse my hair
and the men could see her shadow beyond their fires,

the crazy woman begging in the dry
flash of stars until the flood came,
too sudden to save her.

# HIGH PLACES

She had studied aerial photographs of high places,
inaccessible plateaus rising thousands of feet
from the desert floor, had read
they were inhabited by weasel, mouse and shrew,
but no one knew how they got there,
so she set out to discover for herself.

There were difficulties, of course,
paths that seemed to ascend
levelled out and returned to the plain,
trails narrowed into deer tracks
and disappeared.

She dozed on the mossy side of trees,
dreaming that she had been in the wilderness
forty years though she had been gone
only two days, and her backpack
seemed to fill with stone tablets.

Somewhere above the tree line
the world changed, there were few mice
and no weasels, but strangers who had no difficulty
making the climb appeared
and pointed out the five states
she should be observing from the peak.

And then she didn't stay as long as she wanted:
just as she thought she might begin to understand
how falcons could light on the hardest rock,
and goats almost live on stone, she looked
on all that lay below and was hungry,
and it was time to think of coming down.

# VESSELS

She plows down the sidewalk,
a great vessel in the July torpor,
a tugboat at her side.
The cargo squirms in the hull
like a huge maggot.
It is eating her wind away.

I wave from the easy shore,
sweet spring of body in tropic air,
"How long to port?"

"Past due—eight days now."
The timbers groan.
"With my first,
I could have sailed a year.
I didn't care."

Her tug urges full-speed ahead.
She lists starboard,
she has no sails for him, no breath.
I watch her skirting shore,
surely tonight port.

My belly taut, vessel empty,
I wave again—
lovesick in drydock.

# THE ROLLER SKATING RINK
## (for my daughter Katy)

Through the double door—
organ blare, shiny floor,
orb of mirrors—
I bring you
into the rumbling remember.

The skates still pinch—
their gray tongues
crushed up under knotted strings,
we force our feet into them.
You can't hear me.

Clutching this roar,
you become the wobbly ballast in the gut,
the ache of shin, the ankle burn,
the screw of small shoes.
I am nothing but the slip of you.

I hung once on a boy so shy
we wrenched hands the whole rink round
without ever speaking.
I twelve, and he twelve too,
sweaty and off-balance
in the wheeling lights,
blisters so many
I could not walk for a week,
so let us stop, let's go home
he never held my hand again.

Little girl, child, daughter,
we have been swirling here
for the eternity I forget,
you and I, and I all pain,
for nothing that glitters has changed
and can't we, please, leave now?

# FITTING ROOM
### (for my daughter Katy)

My mother loved me in my green prom dress,
her favorite color, but I will love you in any shade,
in the third grade it was always purple,

and I am watching your white socks now
as in the fitting room next to you, a girl,
your age, is stepping into a red prom dress.

Her feet are sweaty and pink on the orange carpet,
wrinkled like yours when you sluff off your shoes,
and somebody's watching her, too, a brother maybe,

a boyfriend slouched in the chair beside me,
Guns 'n Roses t-shirt, denim jacket,
picking his teeth, chewing his nails,

and as you appear in white linen, she opens
her door too, her eyes begging him
to love it, her hair defiant—

red is not her color, nor is blonde,
and he grunts up and shuffles towards her,
touches her bare shoulder with one hand and shrugs.

She shuts the door, taffeta whispering
to her hand, and he leans forward seeing more
than a red dress dropping at her feet,

while you are showing me your second choice,
pink and cotton, you are so much thinner than you
    were,
and I'll buy either, I'll buy both.

I am thinking how beautiful your hair is,
its own soft color, and when she shows him
the second dress, black, he stands, twirls her around,

his hands clumsy on her blemished back,
and then I want her to be beautiful as you,
whom no one has told what to wear,
and no one has yet asked to dance.

# MOVING OUT

My son just moved out of the house and into the car.
He took his research paper on Neanderthal man
(the one about bicuspid deterioration),
his college application, and the water pik.
"Mom," he says, "a man's gotta do what he's gotta
    do."
He wants the stereo too,
and all the *Richard Wagner* tapes
but there are limits.

"You're only sixteen," I say.
"You don't even have your learner's permit,"
but he keeps reminding me there's a backlog at
    Hopewell High,
and he'll get his driver's training in September.

When I drive to the grocery store,
I find pumpernickel bagels molding in the glove
    compartment
and pineapple cream cheese on the steering wheel.
His stuffed iguana swings fom the rear view mirror.
At night I watch him sit out there
reading *The Origin of Species*.
Doesn't he know he's running down the batteries?
"Read by moonlight," I say, "that's how Piltdown did
    it,
use a kerosene lantern,"
but he keeps muttering things about squatter's rights,
eminent domain and hunter-gatherers.

The backseat has begun to smell like him.
I need some *Renuzit*—
He's out in the parking lot now,
typing his treatise on *homo erectus*.

# REST STOP, MEMORIAL DAY, 1990

Inside, a girl on the phone has been waiting
an hour, Mom, he hasn't come, green mascara
panicking as we pass, and in the rest room
an old woman pats her eyelids with a wadded towel.

I think of our daughter calling,  my mother
weeping for no reason, but this is just a rest stop on
    84
and the floor is dirty.  I hold my handbag in my teeth,
someone has removed the hooks from the stall.

Back in the lobby the soda machine lacks ice,
and I wonder why it eats your quarters and not my
    dimes.
We share a paper cup of soda, and a thin
woman in red shorts asks us for exit 15.

No one behind the desk to help us,
but the man filling the orange drink machine
says those aren't exit numbers on the map,
what city does she want anyway, she looks so lost.

The girl on the phone has begun whimpering,
as if her voice were clotting in her throat, they made
    plans
last night, he was to meet her here at 9:30,
and the woman in red shorts thinks it's Norwalk she
    wants.

I want to tell them both before I leave, don't be afraid,
sometimes people don't show up, birds get lost
    between trees,
cats find new nests, sons abandon Pontiacs,
daughters come home another way, Boston isn't far.

But outside someone has abandoned a half-drunk
    gallon of iced tea

on the asphalt, and at a phone booth along the
    concrete wall
another girl, older than our own, is saying that she is
    staying here
to work on a computer program, and they're to have a
    nice time.

She smiles, hangs up, runs to her little red car where
    someone
is waiting in hiking boots, and you want to walk a
    little and smoke
before we travel on.  In the trash can, a blue spiral
    notebook,
University of Connecticut, American History 101.

# THE CLARITY OF DECEIT
### (for Stan)

The innocent young men,
the ones who wrap themselves in shyness like a sheet,
write poems of prostitutes and sodden kisses
and "with the clarity of deceit"
chide cheap love.

They slip their easy lines to me,
the quick cash of my profession,
red lights pleading,
"Show this to no one."

Underneath the lamp I read
late into my night
the white hot of the hooked regular:
it is raining again and again,
in the streets of Brest;
a man and a woman lie together
in some dark room with dirty linen
while outside the lampdark sputters.

These tawdry slips of speculation,
my pure young writers,
become the price we pay.
The dear conceits
for all our art
lie here
in the lucid dark:

a trick now and then,
one one-day-stand
in some sultry classroom,
turns all for the moment
clear and familiar.

# ENDYMION

At her desk the young man holds out
what he has written, and his hand
seems so suddenly beautiful
she wants to hold it to her mouth,

but what can she speak of this?
Aphrodite has hung her wrinkled breasts
upon a rib and her thin hair rides
the varicose shell,

how we despise old women
who love anything young and beautiful—
and in a passion so incomplete—
it is only the hand she loves.

All that is lovely she can not have.
All that she can not have, she must keep.
She foams ashore like a rotten fish,
where can she lay him in all this sand?

There must be a hillside somewhere,
a place where an old hag comes new
and a boy lies a long time in the moonlight
his white shirt open at the neck,

and his hand his hand
curled as if round a rock.

## "I'M GONNA DRIVE SOMEWHERE FAR"
### (for Karen, a student)

"I'm gonna drive somewhere far
with the windows down
and the music up"

and I'm gonna stretch my ankles
under the dashboard
all the toe to Tallahassee
and I'm gonna fly my velvet hair
the left hand lane
from Phoenix to Kalamazoo
like the flag that never flew
over your blackboard, teacher

Oh, I'll make a turn or two
around the parking lot
so you can hear the asphalt screeching
and never think again
I loved this place
even for a mile

and all asound the long highway
I'm not gonna yield
my goodbyes once
to those exhausting rooms
where you stopped the windows up
and held the music down
so that I never could
look
and
listen

## "AND THESE FEW PRECEPTS"
### (to my graduating seniors)

I know virtue and a few dusty words
on borrowing and lending will not keep
you safe in Boston Paris Wittenburg
Syracuse New York Baltimore Rome,

that I am foolish as Polonius,
trying to pack a thousand vulgar things
into your skull before you leave—how clay
is clay and night is night. You should not listen.
You should laugh and leave and travel light.

    Wit is short, we live
at the end of easily severed threads:

You lean on the willow slant the dark stream,
tossing in stones, leaves, you dabble in dark
waters, you dangle silver barbs as if
all you could catch were radiant fish.

I do not pretend you hang on my words:
you are moving downstream dropping your lines
as you go, and I am left in the sharp air,
a hundred tiny hooks tearing at my tongue.

# TO DAVID, A STUDENT

You slouched through *The Scarlet Letter*
and *Moby Dick,* with the rest of us,
that junior year in high school,

too bored I thought to join the jocks
estimating the length and prick
of that white whale's humdrum,

but when we touched *A Member of the Wedding,*
you wrote about your loneliness:  someone you
     missed,
weekends in New York, a drum and bugle corps.

When you began losing weight your senior year,
we had just begun to hear of that new infection
as full of mortality as any monotonous novel.

You permed your hair. You ironed your pink shirts.
Sometimes the girls beside you sat and stared.
In April you disappeared.

Some days as I hand back dull essays
I hope someone will raise his hand
and tell me where you are, David Frederick Matson,

and whether you will ever come back
with some tedious story
about how you got through all this.

# LAZARUS

It happens like this—
you're waltzing down the sidewalk
past Weltschmerz's Chutzpa Parlour
when the door flams open like a tomb,
and a man in a green bowler comes forth,
and he calls you a "Schmuck!"

You crumple to the sidewalk, an empty candy
    wrapper,
and if a sanitation engineer doesn't scoop you up
with the moldy buns from Johnny's Hot Dog Stand,
you are still lying there wedged between a crack and a
    roach.

But since you are the fortunate sort,
you get collected at dawn, trucked away, thrown over,
    washed up,
after a day or a two, on Mama Earth's Sweet Beach
where no one swims, and you notice after three or
    four hours
in the stinking sun that you can see into your belly.
There's a Coke bottle where your navel used to be
and you raise yourself up on your elbows and peer in.
It's clean to your kidneys.

Your live-in lover ambles by,
asking what brought you so low
that you must lie in the sand with clorox bottles and
    sanitary shells,
and you say, don't worry, the scientists say
that hot love can't co-exist in cold slime.
It's perfectly safe.

He asks again, was it the man around the corner,
the one with a trachiotomy, did he breathe on you.
Was it the the boy in the bunged-up tricycle
who was always running up your heels?
He can not imagine such things happen in a just
    universe.

Night comes and four humpback whales slouch to
    shore
where they pipe the Halleluiah Chorus just as the
    moon rises
over Mortimer's Crematorium.
You are hungry, but the sushi washed up
in a Himalayan Hamburger Box is burnt.
At midnight the stars begin to smell of freon.

At dawn, a nun from the convent at Novina Supina
    swaggers across the sand
and asks you if you've seen a congregation of gulls.
You tell her to unscrew the sunscreen around her neck
    and pour a little down your throat,
it will not do to burn your liver with so little ozone
    left.
She bends over you, her eye to the lip of your navel
and watches the yellow liquid coat your peritoneum.
Just like the commercial, she says, so nice, so very
    nice,
too many priests eat tripe.

You rise from the sand, reconstituted, and crab down
    the shore,
dragging the lining of your stomach in your wake.

# DRYOPE

How easily we walk into terror:
a young woman swings her child
to a freckled shoulder and stoops to pluck a lotus—
the stalk drips blood.

There is none to warn that women become trees:
the child drops from her arms like a leaf,
the husband begs her to speak,
the tongue is a wooden spoon.

How can she answer when his voice
is no more than one branch scraping another?
How can he pretend
she is still flesh and milk at her center?

He clings to her as men cling to trees,
tasting the bark and moss and locust skin,
hanging on her body like a branch dangling from a
     roof,
like a caterpillar who can not shake his silk.

He shadows around her as if she were a sacred grove,
he brings the child to dance in her darkness,
he counts the rings that were his heartwood,
he burns and burns as she grows cold.

## ARS MORIENDI

Last May my neighbor's van settled down
on cement blocks without a word,

and this August his lawn mower,
after no end of noise, silently begged to rust in peace.

I don't know how long
his refrigerator has been squatting

on the front porch
waiting to come in.  As I pass,

I think how polar bears melt into plastic lumps
and apples shrink to porcelain.

Such patience in inanimate things.
Slugs drown their morrows all too quickly in my gin.

The neighbors are complaining though,
it's October and the crab-apples are bombing

his five white sinks
set in a mortal row,

and today he's parked his pick-up
in the front mud for good,

*(Would you look at it?*
*The street's a dump)*

and won't I join them
in some ordinance against slow decay?

# NOTHING CAN BE RUSHED

Nothing can be rushed: a child's hair plaits mornings,
a silk knot tangles days; a shawl weaves thread by
    thread and the nail
that hammered the loom was bent on the birthday of
    iron;
the pin feather begins the yolk, and the egg
you stole from the top of the haystack
chicks at the bottom, history cracks
in the slide to straw.  I suck minutes into my mouth
and spit out eons, the iron scorches a cotton summer,
a plastic cup dies more slowly than dinosaurs.
Everything we do has taken all the time there is.

# THE BACKWARDNESS OF THINGS

The backwardness of things: the way a flame
can shrivel into a safety match;
blood return to its wound; leaves lift up
to their branches and, after a sun,
shy back into buds. We know this happens
but how can we predict the morning
we will lapse into love, anger no more
than a heart fluttering in our hands,
a bird banging its feathers
against our fingers, begging for wings.

## ROOMING WITH WOMEN

I have lived with men so long I have forgotten
the fatness of women, the bulge of belly,
the Rubens thigh, the deep-sunken navel.
I have forgotten the way some women move,
content with their bodies, lying down
on their beds and drawing up their knees
to powder their crotches, how carefully they
anoint themselves with balms and lotions.
I have forgotten that some women languor
in their nakedness, like men who talk to you
in their skin, resting a leg on a chair
and bending an elbow on a knee.
My sister always lifted her breasts
as she dried them after her bath,
amazed at their lucky roundness
in a family of women whose legs were too short
and whose necks were too thin.

## WINSLOW HOMER'S *TWO BIRDS SHOT IN FLIGHT*

How beautiful their bodies hang in air:
lovers hovering home from a party,
sons swinging ropeless from a roof,
daughters slung on invisible hammocks,
sun circling their unkissed skin.

How often we have held our breath:
Paola and Francesca caught in the updraft,
the temperate crows in a Prussian sky, Achilles
holding his heel to the raw umber,
Icarus plunging indigo.  When have swans
not slept on drunken feathers?

The mallard on the left could still be flying:
wings spreading to the reeds, bill pointing home.
The other is dead:   wings crimped, web closed.
See how her neck breaks towards the one white wave,
how she could fall from him in any world
less composed than this.

# WHITSUNTIDE

I could be this old hag just ditched from a bicycle, still
    dog- dizzy on her own heat,
or I could be St. Francis coasting down Linvale Road,
habit flapping to the wind
like the loose wing of a charred crow,

for I have been pumping high up in the Sourland
    Mountains where no one goes alone—
not many birds to preach to, no bear, no boar, no
    wolves,
only the gravid doe
skittering across the road on astonished hooves.

I have been listening with such rushing joy
to the wind licking through the ash,
to the oak lifting up its leaves,
to the sun rending bark and branch and face,

I have been watching the light cleave the wild grapes,
I have been rooting, saint and sow, god and goat,
I have taken so many tree tops with cloven tongues,
that even I now comprehend

how I burn and burn
without belief.

## ABOUT THE AUTHOR

Lois Marie Harrod's fourth book of poetry *Part of the Deeper Sea* was published by Palanquin Press, University of South Carolina—Aiken in 1997, and her chapbook *This Is a Story You Already Know* by Palanquin Press in June, 1999. Her poems have appeared in many journals among them *American Poetry Review, The Carolina Quarterly, Southern Poetry Review, American Pen, Prairie Schooner, The Literary Review, Zone 3* and *Green Mountains Review.* Her earlier publications include the books *Every Twinge a Verdict* (Belle Mead Press, 1987), *Crazy Alice* (Belle Mead Press, 1991 and 1999) and a chapbook *Green Snake Riding* (New Spirit Press, 1994). She received 1992-3 and 1998 fellowships from the New Jersey Council of the Arts for her poetry. She teaches high school English and is the Supervisor of Creative Writing at the New Jersey Governor's School of the Arts. She and her husband Lee Harrod live in Hopewell, New Jersey.

Cover Art: *The Reptilian Brain,* Katherine E. Harrod
Author Photo: Ann Holt

This book was designed by Arrowleaf Balsamroot. It is set in Garamond type and manufactured by Bookcrafters.